A broken egg . . .

"It's not funny, Jess." I wiped my eyes. "My egg is completely ruined." I picked up a piece of the pale green shell.

"Your egg—" Jessica was trying to say something, but all she could do was laugh. "Elizabeth, I always knew you were an egghead in school, but I never knew you were one at home, too," she finally sputtered.

I was getting mad. "It's not very nice to call me names!" I cried.

"Egghead," she kept repeating. "Look—in—mirror," she managed to choke out between giggle fits.

"You're crazy," I said. I marched over to the dresser to look at myself in the mirror. "If it will make you happy—" I stopped.

I reached up to touch the top of my head. There, tangled in my hair, was a fuzzy little chick.

S0-EIC-472

Bantam Books in the SWEET VALLEY KIDS series

SWEET VALLEY KIDS
SUPER SPECIAL

ELIZABETH HATCHES AN EGG

Written by
Molly Mia Stewart

Created by
FRANCINE PASCAL

Illustrated by
Ying-Hwa Hu

BANTAM BOOKS
NEW YORK · TORONTO · LONDON · SYDNEY · AUCKLAND

To Emily Eve Groopman

RL 2, 005-008

ELIZABETH HATCHES AN EGG

A Bantam Book / March 1996

*Sweet Valley High® and Sweet Valley Kids® are
registered trademarks of Francine Pascal*

Conceived by Francine Pascal

*Produced by Daniel Weiss Associates, Inc.
33 West 17th Street
New York, NY 10011*

Cover art by Susan Tang

*All rights reserved.
Copyright © 1996 by Francine Pascal.
Cover art and interior illustrations copyright © 1996 by
Daniel Weiss Associates, Inc.
No part of this book may be reproduced or transmitted
in any form or by any means, electronic or mechanical,
including photocopying, recording, or by any information
storage and retrieval system, without permission in
writing from the publisher.
For information address: Bantam Books.*

If you purchased this book without a cover, you should be aware
that this book is stolen property. It was reported as "unsold and
destroyed" to the publisher and neither the author nor the publisher has
received any payment for this "stripped book."

ISBN: 0-553-48340-4

Published simultaneously in the United States and Canada

Bantam Books are published by Bantam Books, a division of Bantam
Doubleday Dell Publishing Group, Inc. Its trademark, consisting of the
words "Bantam Books" and the portrayal of a rooster, is registered in the
U.S. Patent and Trademark Office and in other countries. Marca
Registrada. Bantam Books, 1540 Broadway, New York, New York 10036.

PRINTED IN THE UNITED STATES OF AMERICA

OPM   0 9 8 7 6 5 4 3 2 1

CHAPTER 1

Springtime Surprises

"Er-er-er-er-ERRR!" I jumped on my sister Jessica's bed and crowed like a rooster. "Come on, sleepyhead. Today's the day we get to visit Marty's farm," I said.

Jessica groaned and pulled the covers over her head.

"Elizabeth Wakefield—go back to bed. It's way too early to get up," she complained.

I hopped out of bed and pulled on my favorite green sweatshirt. "I smell cinnamon toast," I said. Jessica loves cinnamon toast for breakfast.

"Umpph," she said.

"Okay, then, I'll eat it all." I hurried to pull on my jeans and brush my hair into a ponytail. I didn't need a mirror to see what I looked like. I just had to look at my sister! Jessica and I are twins. We are identical, from our long blond hair and our blue-green eyes, to the dimple we each have in our left cheek. We're both in the same second-grade class at Sweet Valley Elementary School.

Jessica and I are best friends, but that doesn't mean we don't have different ideas about things. *I'd* been looking forward all week to our visit to Mom's old friend's farm.

I skipped into the kitchen and gave Mom a big kiss. "I can't wait to go to Marty's farm."

"And I know she can't wait for you to come, either," Mom said.

Jessica wandered into the kitchen,

stretching and yawning. "I *can* wait," she said. "I'll probably get my new shoes all dirty."

"Then don't wear them!" I said impatiently.

"But they go with my outfit," she said.

"I don't think the cows will care," I told her. Jessica made a face at me, then took a bite of her cinnamon toast.

An hour later, Mom, Jessica, and I drove to Marty's farm.

"There it is!" I pointed to a big wooden sign. HAPPY DALE FARM, it read.

Marty was waiting in the yard, waving to us.

"Hi, Marty!" Mom, Jessica, and I said, running up the driveway.

"Hi, everyone," Marty said. "I'm glad you could come." She gave us each a big hug.

"There are so many animals here," I said gleefully.

"Springtime brings surprises on a farm," Marty said. "I have lots of new babies for you to meet."

Jessica crinkled her nose as we stepped inside the cool, dark barn. "P-U!" she said.

Marty laughed. "I forget that city noses aren't used to country smells."

Marty led us beyond the barn to the sheep pen. "My ewe, Tilly, had twins yesterday," she said.

"Ewe?" I asked.

"That's what we call female sheep."

I peeked over the fence. Tilly lay in the middle of the pen. I could see two little tails wagging in back of her.

"Come on. You'll need to see them better to come up with names," Marty said as she opened the gate.

"Names?" asked Jessica.

"Sure." Marty smiled. "It's a good idea for twins to name twins, don't you think?" she said, winking at us.

I walked slowly over to the open gate, with Jessica hiding behind me. "She's awfully big!" I said as the sheep looked at us with her big brown eyes.

Suddenly Tilly bleated loudly. "Baaaahhhh!"

"Oh!" Jessica said. She jumped and ran back to Mom.

"She won't hurt you. She's just telling you to be careful with her babies," Marty said, laughing. She picked up one of the lambs and laid it in my arms. It was soft and warm and smelled of sweet grass.

"Don't be afraid, Jess," I said. "It's like holding a cloud!"

Jessica edged forward slowly. Marty brought her the other lamb.

"I've got a great name for this one," I said. "How about Bo-peep, from the nursery rhyme?"

"Baa!" Bo-peep answered.

"I think she likes it," said Marty.

Jessica stared at the lamb in her arms.

"Then this little one must be Mary!"

"Perfect names!" said Marty. "I knew I could count on you."

"Baahh!" Tilly bleated again.

We walked out of the barnyard and Marty closed the gate behind us.

Near the house, Marty showed us a huge chicken coop.

"I've got Rhode Island Reds, Leghorns, and Golden Comets. Annie's my favorite," Marty said, pointing to a plump little chicken. "She's more like a pet than a chicken. She's an Arcauna and lays her own Easter eggs. They are the prettiest green you've ever seen."

"Can I see one of her eggs?" I asked.

"Annie hides her nest so I can't find it," said Marty. "If we did find it, she might get upset. Then she'd leave her eggs, and they wouldn't hatch."

Jessica pointed to a sign on the chicken coop. It read $1 FOR 1 DOZEN. "Do you sell eggs, too?" she asked.

Marty nodded.

"Oh, Mom, please buy some," begged Jessica. "Then we'll have plenty to decorate for the school Easter egg-decorating contest."

Mom agreed, and we all went into Marty's cheerful kitchen, where we had homemade gingerbread and lemonade.

After a while, Mom looked at her watch. "Goodness, we'd better be going."

I jumped up. "Do we have time for one last look at the animals?" I asked.

Mom nodded.

I ran out and said good-bye to Tilly, Bo-peep, and Mary.

As I passed the chicken coop, something caught my eye in the grass. It was a beautiful green egg!

I ran back to the house. "I found a green egg!" I yelled. Mom, Jessica, and Marty came with me to look.

"I bet this rolled off Annie's nest. She

won't take it back, now," Marty said. She picked up the pale green egg. "Here. This can be a souvenir of your visit."

I picked up the egg. It was a lovely speckled green color. It was definitely a special egg. Marty was right—springtime did bring surprises!

CHAPTER 2

Egg-straordinary Egg

When I woke up the next morning, the first thing I did was check on my egg. It was safe and sound under my pillow. After getting dressed, I carried my egg down to the kitchen. Our biggest pot boiled away on the stove, and the counter was covered with bowls of different colors of dye.

"What's going on in here?" I asked.

Jessica was dashing back and forth. "Egg decorating, what does it look like?" she asked.

"It looks like you crashed into a rainbow!" I said. Jessica's hands and face were streaked with all different colors of dye.

Jessica looked at her arms. "Do you think this stuff washes off?" she asked.

"Don't worry," I said. "If it doesn't, you can always enter yourself in the egg-decorating contest. I'm sure you'd win a prize."

"She'll win the prize for making the biggest mess," our big brother Steven said as he came into the kitchen.

Jessica made a goofy face. "Here, Steven, let me give you a big hug!"

"Don't touch me!" Steven yelled, running away from her. "You'll turn me all yellow and pink!" They skidded around the table, laughing.

"Hey, slow down there," Mom said. "You might break something."

"Yeah, like my egg," I said. I hugged it closer to me.

"It might be a good idea to hard boil that egg," Mom said to me. "That way, it won't make such a mess if it breaks."

"No way!" I stepped back. Eggs could crack while they were cooking. I didn't want to take a chance on ruining my perfect green egg.

"Hey, if you don't boil it, it might even hatch," Steven said.

"But we don't know if the egg is fertilized or not," Mom said. "So it's probably just a pretty egg."

"It's a beautiful egg. And I've got a plan to keep it safe and sound," I told Mom. "If Steven will give me one of his old tennis socks."

"Sure, I've got tons of them," Steven said, running up to his room.

"I want a nice clean one!" I called after him.

Jessica held her nose. "The only things that smell worse than Marty's barn are

Steven's dirty socks!" she said, giggling.

Steven came back into the room. "What are you going to do with this?" he asked, handing me a sock.

"I'll show you," I said. I slipped Annie's egg inside. It was a perfect fit.

"It looks like you've made a coat for your egg," Mom said.

"I'm not done yet," I told her.

While Steven and Jessica went back to dyeing their eggs, I rummaged in the ragbag for one of Dad's old ties. Using some fabric scraps, Mom and I stitched a pocket to the front of the tie. Then, I slipped Steven's sock into the pocket. "Would you tie the ends behind me?" I asked Mom.

"Oh, I see what it is," Steven said. "An egg cradle!"

"This egg is so beautiful, I'm going to enter it in the egg-decorating contest," I said.

"You can't do that," Jessica said.

"Because Annie the chicken decorated it, not you."

"I'll figure out something," I told her. "The rules don't say you have to color the egg. Especially if it's already colored!"

Jessica reached over and put her hand on my forehead. "You feel like an egg," she said.

"What do you mean?" I asked.

"You've finally cracked!" she said.

"Instead of decorating my egg, I'm going to decorate *around* my egg," I said. "I'll make a diorama."

I ran upstairs and I gathered up some construction paper, glue, magazines, and an old shoe box. I laid out my supplies on the dining room table.

I cut some trees out of green and brown paper and I made a barn out of red construction paper. Then I glued them inside the shoe box.

Mom found some blue cellophane in a drawer, and I cut it into the shape of a lake. Next, I cut pictures of farm animals out of magazines. I glued them onto Popsicle sticks and stuck them around the barn.

"Now for the best part," I said. I went out to the garage and collected some of the straw Marty had given us for our garden. With a tiny bit of Mom's help, I shaped it into a nest. It was just the right size for my egg.

Jessica studied my diorama. "The nest looks real! Let's see how it looks with the egg in it." She reached for my egg cradle.

I stepped back. "I'll do it," I said. I carefully slipped the egg out of the cradle and placed it into the nest.

"That looks great, Lizzie," Jessica said. She patted my egg gently.

"Mom, what do you think?" I asked.

"I'd say that it looks *egg*-straordinary!" she said.

16

CHAPTER 3

An Egg-ceptional Day

The next morning, I got out of bed and put my egg into my sock drawer. I wanted to keep it safe while I got ready for school.

Jessica peeked out from under her covers. "Don't tell me you slept with that thing again!" she said. "The next thing you know, you'll want chicken feed for breakfast."

"Cluck, cluck." I made chicken sounds and scratched at the floor with my feet.

"Very funny," Jessica said, throwing back her covers. "Promise me you won't tell Lila about this. She'll think I'm weird if she finds out my sister sleeps with a chicken."

"An egg is *not* the same thing as a chicken," I said. I dressed, then slipped the egg into the egg cradle.

We went downstairs and had breakfast. Jessica admired the rows of eggs she had decorated.

"Which egg do you think I should bring for the contest?" Jessica asked me.

"These two eggs are my favorites," I said, pointing to a pink egg and an egg with blue flowers. "Why don't you ask Dad which one he'd vote for?"

"Dad, which egg do you think I should enter into the school egg contest? This one—" Jessica picked up the pink egg.

Dad poured his coffee. "That's pretty," he said.

"—or this one?" Jessica asked, reaching for the one with the blue flowers.

As she lifted it up, it slipped out of her hand. *Crunch.*

"Oh, no!" Jessica stared at her cracked egg on the floor.

"I liked the pink one better, anyway," Dad said.

"Yuck!" Jessica said.

"I guess we forgot to hard boil that one," Mom said.

I made a promise to myself never to let Jessica hold *my* egg. I didn't want it to end up on the floor!

When we got to school we saw a crowd gathered around Lila Fowler and her egg.

"Is that *real* gold?" someone asked Lila.

"Yes. Fourteen-karat gold," Lila said, holding her egg up. "Daddy took it to a jewelry store and they covered it with gold leaf. It's like paint made out of gold." Lila put the egg back into its velvet carrying case. "It's very expensive," she said.

Jessica looked at her pink egg. "You poor thing," she said. "You don't stand a chance against a real gold-painted egg."

"I think you have a good chance," I told her. "Especially since you decorated it yourself, and didn't pay someone to decorate it for you."

"Thanks, Elizabeth," Jessica said. She smiled at me and grabbed my hand. "Let's go see what the other kids in our class brought!"

Our teacher, Mrs. Otis, was standing in the doorway to our room, greeting everybody. When I stepped inside, I couldn't believe my eyes—our classroom looked like it had been taken over by the Easter Bunny!

We admired all the different eggs displayed on the counter.

"Look at Andy Franklin's egg!" Jessica exclaimed. It was covered with bug stickers. "It's not exactly Easter-ish."

I smiled. "Maybe not," I said, "but it

looks just like the kind of egg Andy would decorate!"

The egg Julie Porter had brought was covered in fancy designs. "How did you do this?" I asked her.

"My grandmother is Ukrainian. She helped me. These kinds of decorations are traditional. They're called *Pysanky,*" Julie explained. She looked at my diorama. "Your egg is a pretty color, too. How did you get that shade of green?"

"Secret ingredient," I said with a smile. Then I told her about Annie.

"Wow—a chicken that lays colored Easter eggs," Julie said, shaking her head. "Wouldn't it be great if there were one that laid chocolate eggs? Yum!"

"Please take your seats, class," Mrs. Otis said. "I know you're all very excited about the Easter egg contest. I've asked some of the other teachers to help me judge. They'll be coming in right before lunch."

21

I looked at all the eggs on the counter. There were so many interesting decorations. But I still thought Annie's egg was the prettiest.

"This is a busy week," Mrs. Otis went on. "Don't forget we also have the Spring pageant and parade afterward on Friday, before the Easter holiday."

Jessica pushed her hair behind her ears. "I'm going to have the best Easter bonnet for this year's parade," she said.

"Wait until you see the hat I'm getting from Paris!" Lila said.

Jessica frowned.

"We need some kids to write a skit for our class," Mrs. Otis said.

Amy Sutton raised her hand. "Elizabeth and I can write the class skit, can't we, Elizabeth?"

I thought about it for a second.

"Come on, Lizzie. You're such a good writer. It should be fun!" Amy said.

Mrs. Otis nodded and smiled.

"Okay," I said.

Miss Johnson, the third-grade teacher, knocked on our classroom door. "Are you ready for us?" she asked. Several other teachers were with her.

I sat up straight in my chair. The teachers walked up and down in front of the counter where the eggs were displayed.

Jessica poked me. "Look," she whispered. Several of the teachers were standing in front of my diorama and talking.

"I can't watch," I said. After a while, Miss Johnson walked over to talk to Mrs. Otis.

"The judges have chosen a winner," Mrs. Otis announced.

"This was a hard job because all the eggs were decorated in such creative ways," Miss Johnson said. "But the prize for the best decorated egg goes to—"

I crossed my fingers. Miss Johnson

glanced over where Jessica and I were sitting.

"Elizabeth Wakefield!" Miss Johnson said.

The whole class started clapping.

I walked to the front of the room. Miss Johnson handed me a huge blue ribbon.

"For Miss Elizabeth Wakefield," she said. "First prize for The Most Egg-ceptional Egg."

CHAPTER 4

Scrambled Sisters

When I got back to my desk, Jessica admired my blue ribbon. "I'm glad you won, Elizabeth. It's almost as good as winning first prize myself!" she said. She reached into the diorama box and started to pick up my egg.

"Just leave it there!" I said. I didn't want it to end up like the egg at home this morning.

Jessica pulled her hands back. "I wasn't going to hurt it. I just wanted to hold it," she said.

"I don't think it's a good idea if too many people hold it," I said.

"Elizabeth, it's *just* an egg!" Jessica exclaimed.

"It's not just an egg," I said. "It's Annie's egg—my special egg—and I don't want anybody else holding it."

Jessica made a face. "You don't need to be so grouchy," she said.

"Well, you don't need to be so grabby," I said. I gently lifted my egg out of the diorama box, put it back into the egg cradle. Jessica stomped back to her seat.

At recess I walked out toward the playground.

"Hey, Elizabeth! Are you going to play soccer with us?" my friend, Todd Wilkins, asked.

"Sure!" I said. As I ran to catch up with Todd, the egg cradle bounced against my chest. I stopped running and called after him, "Go ahead without me. I don't think I'd better play today." I knew my egg might break from all the bouncing. Or, even worse, get smashed by the soccer ball.

"You're not going to wear that thing all day, are you?" asked Todd.

Jessica skipped by with Lila and Ellen Riteman. "I offered to hold it for her, but she wouldn't let me," she said. She made a face at me. "Come on, you guys. Let's go have some fun." They ran off.

I sat by the long wall and watched my friends play. It's not nearly as much fun to watch soccer as it is to play it. Even Jessica's jump rope game began to look inviting. And I don't even like to jump rope! I sighed, then patted my egg. "I'd rather take good care of you than play with those guys, anyway," I said. But a recess can seem very long and boring when you're just watching other kids play.

Don't forget what happened this morning, I reminded myself. *It would be horrible if Jessica got a hold of Annie's egg. It'd end up broken for sure.*

Jessica came up to me as soon as recess was over. "Can I please hold your egg now?" she asked.

I shook my head.

"Elizabeth, you are so mean," Jessica said. "I don't see why you won't give me even one little turn. I thought we were best friends."

"We are, but—"

"But your egg is more important than being nice to your own sister?" Jessica asked. I could tell by her tone of voice that she really felt hurt. But I felt responsible for Annie's egg.

When I didn't answer, Jessica frowned at me.

"You'll be sorry, Elizabeth Wakefield," she said in an angry voice, and walked away.

I thought Jessica was going to leave me alone, but I was wrong. After the spelling quiz, she reached over and tried to grab the egg cradle from me!

"Let go!" I yelled. Annie's egg nearly fell out of the egg cradle. "This is my egg, and I don't want you to touch it!" I shouted.

Mrs. Otis hurried over. "Elizabeth!" she scolded. "This is so unlike you."

I hid my face in my spelling workbook.

"Let's step out in the hall for a minute," Mrs. Otis said.

Jessica snickered.

"You, too, Jessica," our teacher said. When we were outside the classroom, Mrs. Otis asked us to explain what had happened.

"I just wanted to hold her egg," Jessica said. Then she turned to me. "Why can't you let me hold it just once?"

"Because I don't want it to get broken, like the egg this morning," I said. My voice was getting loud again.

"Girls, girls," Mrs. Otis said. "Let's

not start fighting again. I think you should both say you're sorry."

"I'm sorry for yelling in class," I told Mrs. Otis.

"And I'm sorry you're so selfish," Jessica said, glaring at me.

"That's enough," Mrs. Otis said. "I think I see what we need to do here. Jessica, you must promise to stop bothering Elizabeth about holding her egg. It *is* very special to her, after all," she said.

Jessica hung her head.

"And, Elizabeth, you must promise not to bring your egg to school anymore."

"But—," I started.

Mrs. Otis raised her eyebrow.

"Okay," I said sadly. "I promise."

"I promise, too," Jessica said.

Since I had made a promise to Mrs. Otis, I had to keep my word. But I sure didn't want to.

CHAPTER 5

Elizabeth the Egghead

"**D**id you notice how good I am at keeping my promise?" Jessica asked after dinner.

"Yes, I did," I said. Jessica hadn't asked to hold my egg again for the rest of the day.

My sister plopped down on the couch next to me. "I'm sorry I was such a pest, Lizzie," she said.

"That's okay," I said.

"How come you still look so sad?" she asked.

"I'm worried about my egg. I don't know where to put it to keep it safe tomorrow," I said. Mom had offered to keep it in the kitchen, but I had said no. What if she forgot it was Annie's egg and used it for dinner or something? I got goose bumps just thinking about that.

I went upstairs to do my homework. A few minutes later, Jessica pranced into our room wearing a huge hat.

"Look what I found in the dress-up trunk!" she said. "Isn't this the perfect Easter bonnet?"

The brim was bent on the side. An ugly orange straw flower the size of a softball sat smack on the front of the hat. Two raggedy green-striped ribbons hung off the back. "It's . . . interesting," I said.

Jessica giggled. "You have to use your imagination, Elizabeth. Wait until I'm done fixing it up," she said. She looked through a box of brightly colored ribbons.

"I'm busy using my imagination to think of a way to take my egg to school tomorrow," I said. I rocked the egg gently in my hands. "I just hate to leave it sitting around here. Who knows what might happen to it!"

"Maybe you could take it in your lunch box. Lots of kids bring eggs in their lunches," she said.

"Green eggs?" I asked.

"I guess you're right," Jessica said. She held up a purple ribbon. "A green egg wouldn't egg-xactly blend in."

"Very funny," I said. It wouldn't be right to sneak my egg to school, anyway, not after I had promised Mrs. Otis.

"Girls," Mom called up the stairs. "Time for bed."

We hopped into our pajamas and got into bed. I put my egg under my pillow. Soon, Jessica was sound asleep. I tossed and turned, trying to think of a safe place to leave my egg while I was at school.

*   *   *

"Wake up, sleepyhead," Jessica called to me in the morning.

I rolled on my back and stretched. Something crunched under my head. "Ouch, what's poking me?" I asked, throwing back the covers. When I saw what was under my pillows, I felt tears stinging my eyes.

"Jessica!" I cried. "You promised to leave my egg alone." Bits of broken green shell were scattered all over the bed.

Jessica stood up. "I didn't touch your silly egg. I promise!"

"Then what's all this?" I asked, showing her the eggshell. My voice was all shaky, and I could hardly swallow over the big lump in my throat.

"I don't know how that happened," Jessica said. Then she got the strangest look on her face and started to laugh.

"It's not funny, Jess." I wiped my eyes. "My egg—Annie's egg—it's completely ruined." I picked up a piece

35

of the beautiful pale green shell.

"Your egg—" Jessica was trying to say something, but all she could do was laugh.

"That's right. My egg," I said, holding up a bit of shell. "At least, it used to be my egg." I wiped away the tears on my cheeks. "This isn't funny, Jessica."

Jessica had dropped to the floor and was rolling back and forth. She kept laughing and pointing. "Elizabeth, I always knew you were an egghead in school, but I never knew you were one at home, too," she finally sputtered.

I was getting mad. "It's not very nice to call me names!" I cried. "Especially at a time like this."

The madder I got, the harder Jessica laughed. "Stop it right now!" I yelled at her.

"Egghead," she kept repeating, pointing at my head. "Look—in—mirror," she barely managed to choke out between giggle fits.

36

"You're crazy," I said. I marched over to the dresser to look at myself in the mirror. "If it will make you happy—" I stopped.

Jessica came to stand behind me, wiping away tears of laughter. "See what I was trying to tell you?"

I reached up to touch the top of my head. There, tangled in my hair, was a fuzzy little chick.

CHAPTER 6

Sneeches

"Oh, my gosh!" I gasped. "I hatched Annie's egg!" I gently pulled the chick out of my hair and cradled it in my hands. "It's as light as a feather," I whispered.

"That's because it *is* all feathers," said Jessica. She was still breathing hard from her laughing fit. She sat down next to me on the bed and reached out to pet the little chick.

"Sneech! Sneech!" it said. It made funny noises and tried to hide in my pajama top.

"It thinks you're its mother," Jessica said.

"Do you really?" I asked the chick. It peeped softly. "Peep, peep," I answered back.

Jessica giggled. "I never knew you spoke chicken," she said.

I grinned. "I didn't, either, but I'm going to have to learn." The chick peeped at me again. "My name is Elizabeth, what's yours?" I asked.

Jessica jumped up and ran downstairs. "Mom, Dad, Steven! Elizabeth hatched her egg!" she yelled.

I stroked the tiny chick. "Don't be scared," I said, using a soft, quiet voice like Marty had used with Tilly at the farm. "I'll take care of you."

The chick snuggled even closer to me.

"I bet if Annie the chicken were here, she'd tuck you under her wing," I said. I didn't have wings, so I tucked the chick into the sleeve of my pajama top.

Some of the chick's feathers were still damp, and I could feel its tiny heart beating fast as I stroked it. "Are you okay, little baby?" I whispered. The noises it was making sounded like happy noises, but it was hard to tell. "I wonder what Annie would do right now," I said. The little chick just looked up at me and blinked.

Mom, Dad, and Steven came running up the stairs. They skidded to a halt by my bed.

"Shhhh!" I scolded. "Don't scare the baby."

Mom shook her head. "Jessica wasn't kidding. You really did hatch that egg!" she said.

"All that time you were trying to keep it safe, you also must have kept it warm enough to hatch," Steven added. "That's pretty cool, Elizabeth."

"What are you going to name it?" Jessica asked.

"Wait, I don't think you should get too attached to the little critter, girls," Dad said. "I haven't said we could keep it."

"But, Dad, Sneeches is so cute and little," I said. "He needs me!"

"Sneeches?" Mom asked.

"Sneech, sneech," Sneeches answered.

"See, he even knows his name," I said.

Dad shook his head. "I agree that he is very cute, but I don't think we can keep him. People don't keep chickens for pets."

"But he's not a chicken. He's a chick," I said. I turned to Mom. "Don't you remember what Marty said about Annie being such a good pet?"

Mom and Dad looked at each other. Sneeches peeped again, and Mom's face softened. But Dad shook his head.

"We can't raise him, Elizabeth. He needs to be on a farm with other chickens," he said.

"But he thinks I'm his mother!" I said. I nuzzled Sneeches's soft downy feathers against my cheek. "And Marty said Annie wouldn't accept any eggs that had fallen out of the nest."

"This is a chick, not an egg," Dad said. "I'm sure Annie will take really good care of him."

"But, Dad, I can't give him up," I said. My eyes welled up with tears.

Dad sat down on the bed with me. "Elizabeth, I know this chick means a lot to you, but we can't keep him. We don't know anything about taking care of chickens," he said.

"But I could learn!" I cried.

Sneeches turned his head this way and that. I knew he was counting on me to be a good mother to him. I couldn't give him up. Not after I'd hatched him!

"But, Dad—," I started.

Mom looked sad. Dad sighed. "I'm sorry, Elizabeth. But on Saturday, we'll have to take Sneeches back to Marty's farm," he said.

Then he turned and left the room.

CHAPTER 7

Mother Hen

Jessica kept an eye on Sneeches while I got dressed for school. Every time I heard Sneeches chirp, I started crying all over again. My nose was redder than strawberry jam.

"I'm sorry you can't keep him. He's so cute!" Jessica said. Sneeches scratched around on my bedspread.

"Even if I only have him for a few days, I'm going to take good care of him," I said, picking Sneeches up. I carried the chick downstairs.

"I called Marty and told her about Sneeches," Mom said. "She was amazed the egg hatched. She said we don't have to feed the chick for thirty-six hours, and after that we can give him chicken mash. She also said it's very important to keep him warm, and suggested using a shoe box. We need to line the bottom with Kitty Litter or something like that."

"I know just the box," I said.

"I'll run down to Caroline Pearce's to borrow some Kitty Litter," Jessica volunteered. Like a flash, she was out the door.

In a few minutes I changed my diorama into a snug little home for Sneeches. I clothespinned part of an old ski sweater over the top of the box so Sneeches could be cozy but still get some air.

"I'm back!" Jessica said as she came tearing into the kitchen. "Caroline said we can have more if we need it." She poured the litter into the bottom of the box. Then I set it near the heater vent in the kitchen so Sneeches could stay warm.

"Looks like Sneeches is all set," Dad said. "Everybody off to school. Have a good day."

"It'd be a better day if I could stay home and take care of Sneeches," I said.

"I'll keep a close eye on him," Mom promised.

"Don't miss the bus," Dad said. We hurried out the door.

By the time we got to school, everyone knew about Sneeches, thanks to blabbermouth Caroline Pearce.

Someone had written ELIZABETH HATCHED AN EGG on the blackboard. Everyone wanted to know every little detail about Sneeches. Finally, Mrs. Otis called a time-out.

"I know you're all very interested in Elizabeth's little chick, but we do have schoolwork to do," Mrs. Otis said. "If you all promise to settle down for your lessons, I promise to allow Sneeches to

47

come for a visit before he leaves for the farm." She glanced at me. "If that's OK with Elizabeth."

"I'd love to bring him to school," I told Mrs. Otis.

The other kids went back to their work, but I couldn't stop thinking about Sneeches. While I numbered my paper for the math test, I wondered whether Sneeches was awake or asleep. While I was supposed to be doing my quiet reading, I wondered whether Sneeches missed me.

At lunchtime, while sitting in my usual spot with Amy and Eva, I wondered what I was going to feed Sneeches. Marty had said Sneeches didn't have to eat for thirty-six hours! But I couldn't just let him go hungry.

"Elizabeth," Amy said, nudging me. "You haven't heard a single word I've said."

"Yes, I did," I said.

"Then what did I just ask you?" Amy asked.

I looked down at my lunch box. "You're right," I admitted. "I was thinking about Sneeches."

Amy sighed. "Well, you have other things you need to think about. Like writing the skit for the Easter Pageant," she said.

"I know," I said.

"How about if you come over to my house after school to work on it?" Amy suggested.

"Not today," I answered. "I've got to get home to take care of Sneeches."

"Then we'll have to do it tomorrow. We don't have much time, Elizabeth," she warned.

"I'll work on it at home tonight," I promised.

After school, Jessica, Steven, and I ran home from the bus stop to check on Sneeches. He was happy to see us.

"Sneech," he called from his little home. "Sneech, sneech."

I bent down and lifted him out. He scratched at the floor and bobbed around.

"He looks like dandelion fuzz on legs," Steven said. We all laughed.

I stood up to get a snack. Sneeches followed me across the kitchen floor.

"He really thinks you're his mother," Jessica said. "That is so cute."

"Poor Sneeches," Steven said, making a sad face. "How awful to have Elizabeth for a mother!"

"Steven!" I said, throwing a grape at him. "Thanks a lot."

"Do you think he's hungry?" he asked. I looked down at Sneeches. He was pecking at the grape that had landed at Steven's feet.

"I don't know if he should eat that. I wish I knew what to feed him until we get the chicken mash," I said. I started to worry again.

"We'll go to the library and get a book on chickens. That should tell us what to feed him," Jessica offered. "Come on, Steven."

While I watched Sneeches, Jessica and Steven took their bikes and went off to the library.

Before I knew it, they were back with a book on chickens. I read every word of the book they had checked out.

"He needs a water dish," I said.

"How about this?" Jessica grabbed a big bowl.

"The book says to use something small, like a jar lid," I said.

"I just happen to have one," Mom said, getting it out for me.

"Now we need some little pebbles to put into it so Sneeches can get real close to get a drink but not get his feet wet," I said.

"I'll be in charge of rocks," Steven said. He dashed outside and was back in a minute with a handful of pebbles.

As soon as the water was set up, I carried Sneeches over to it. He dipped his tiny beak in, then tilted his head back.

"He knows just what to do!" I said. I felt so proud of my smart little Sneeches.

I spent the afternoon doing everything the book said to take care of him. Before I knew it, it was dinnertime.

"Hi, everybody!" Dad said when he got home from work. He was carrying a package wrapped in plain brown paper.

"What's that?" I asked.

"Oh, it's nothing," Dad said, looking embarrassed. He hid the package behind his back.

"Is it a present for me?" Jessica asked.

"No, it's not for you," Dad said.

"It's my new baseball glove," Steven guessed.

"No, it's not a baseball glove." Dad's cheeks turned pink.

"Tell us, Dad," I said. "What's in there?"

He handed me the package. "It's mash—baby chick food—for Sneeches," he mumbled.

"Oh, Dad, thanks!" I said. I unwrapped the package and poured the feed into a little dish.

Dad picked up the newspaper. "Well, we want to deliver a healthy chick to Marty," he said. He buried his nose in the sports page. I jumped up and gave him a hug.

"Elizabeth, grab Sneeches!" Jessica called. "He's running across the kitchen!"

I caught Sneeches just before he squeezed behind the refrigerator. I followed him around the whole evening. I watched to make sure he didn't fall off the steps or get stuck under the couch.

When he finally went to sleep for the night, I collapsed on my bed. I was tired.

Jessica yawned and closed her math book.

"Oh, no," I said, clapping my hand to my head. "I forgot to do my homework."

"You were awfully busy with Sneeches," Jessica said. "Did you even work on the class skit?"

"I forgot to do that, too," I said. I hadn't done anything I was supposed to do that night, except take care of Sneeches. Being a mother hen was hard work!

CHAPTER 8

Hide-and-Seek Sneeches

The next morning I had the weirdest dream. It was time for school, and I was trying to get dressed, but none of my clothes fit me. Jessica held out my favorite green sweatshirt, but I couldn't get it on over my wings. Wings? Also in the dream I kept hearing funny noises, like a bird chirping somewhere. It wasn't chirping exactly, though. It was more like "sneeching."

"Oh, my goodness!" I said. I sat straight up, wide awake. It wasn't a dream. Sneeches was on my pillow, blinking at me.

"How did you get out of your box?" I said.

"Sneech, sneech."

I laughed. "So, you're not going to tell me your secret, huh?" I asked. Sneeches hopped out of my hand and ran around on the bedspread.

"Oh, it's so early," I said, yawning. "Can you go back to sleep?" Sneeches just peeped louder.

My eyes were blurry as I got him fresh food and water. "Your mommy is very tired this morning," I told him. It was hard to be cranky at Sneeches, though. He was so cute.

He pecked and scratched in my sock drawer. "Oh, you want me to wear *these* socks today?" I asked, pulling out my green-and-white-striped ones.

"Sneech!" Sneeches said.

I set him down on the floor, and he followed me to the closet. "OK, then, which outfit should I wear?" I asked.

He scratched the floor under my favorite green overalls.

"Hey, we have the same good taste!" I said with a giggle. "Is this shirt okay?" I held it out for Sneeches to inspect. He pecked at it a few times. "That must mean yes," I said. Getting ready for school had never been this much fun before Sneeches.

I sat down on the bed to put on my shoes. I tied the right one on, then reached for the left. It was full of fuzzy chick.

"That's not really your size," I said, laughing. I gave Sneeches a ride down to the kitchen in my sneaker.

"Good morning, Elizabeth," Dad said. He poured Mom some coffee as she read the newspaper.

"Good morning, Elizabeth *and* Sneeches," Mom corrected. She held out her hands. I gave her the chick. "What a sweet little thing you are," Mom cooed.

Dad tried to act like he wasn't interested, but I noticed he stopped to pet Sneeches every so often as he finished getting ready for work.

"Hey, it's my turn to play with Sneeches!" Steven said as he hurried into the kitchen. He scooped Sneeches up.

Mom pretended to look shocked. "I can't believe this. Steven is actually letting something come between him and his breakfast. This is a first!"

"I never knew a chick could be so much fun," Steven said.

We were all talking about Sneeches and his cute little antics when Jessica came down to the kitchen wearing her bonnet.

"Nice hat, Jessica," Steven said with a laugh.

"Uh, are you going to wear that to school?" Dad asked, looking up from his papers.

Jessica tossed her head. "Don't be silly, Dad. It's not ready yet," she said.

Dad looked relieved and went back to his papers.

"Is that your Easter bonnet for the parade at school?" Mom asked.

"It will be," Jessica said. She took it off her head and held it out to Mom. "I mean, you do think I can fix this up, don't you, Mom?"

Mom gulped. "Certainly I do. It's going to take some time and creativity, that's all," she said.

"That's what I think, too," Jessica said. She fingered the frayed green ribbon. "I mean, all it needs are some fresh ribbons, something else instead of this ugly flower, and—"

"And a fairy godmother to make it all happen," Steven interrupted.

"Thanks a lot!" Jessica said and stuck her tongue out at him.

Mom wrapped her arm around Jessica's shoulder. "I'm sure there are some things you could use in that trunk full of old dress-up clothes. We can check in there after school," she said.

"It'll turn out great, Jess," I said, trying to sound encouraging. "You're good at dressing up old clothing."

"I am, aren't I?" Jessica said, turning the hat around in her hands.

"Speaking of being good at things, watch this!" Steven said. He wiggled his finger across the floor like a worm. Sneeches ran after it, pecking and chirping. "He has another trick, too!" Steven bragged. He put his head back and crowed like a rooster. "Cock-a-doodle-doo!"

"Sneech, sneech, sneech," peeped Sneeches.

"See, he's trying to imitate me!" Steven said.

"That's very interesting, Steven," Mom said. "But now you need to eat your breakfast or you'll be late for school."

"Speaking of being late, I've got to go

61

or I'll be late to the office. Good-bye, everybody," Dad said. He scooped up the last of his papers, grabbed his briefcase, and ran out the door. I heard his car pull out of the driveway.

Suddenly, we heard his horn honking. We all went running outside.

"Is something wrong?" Mom called.

Dad rolled down the window and pointed inside his car. There on the front seat with him was Sneeches.

"How'd he get in there?" I asked.

"He must have hitched a ride in my briefcase," Dad said. "I've carried a lot of things in this old case, but never a chicken!"

I reached in and picked Sneeches up. "Now he knows one more trick—how to play hide-and-seek!" I said.

We all laughed.

CHAPTER 9

... Starring Sneeches!

As soon as we got to school, Lila and Ellen came running up to us.

"Guess what?" Lila said breathlessly. "My hat came yesterday! It is *so* fashionable."

"Oh?" Jessica's voice sounded annoyed. "How nice."

"Nice?" Ellen said. "It's more than nice."

Lila nodded.

"So you've seen it already?" Jessica asked Ellen.

Ellen shook her head. "Not yet, but if it's from Paris, it has to be fancy!" she said.

Lila walked a few feet, acting like she was a model in a fashion show. "Jessica, you can't believe how beautiful it is. It has feathers and scarves all over it," Lila said. "What does your Easter bonnet look like?"

Jessica's mouth opened and then closed. She looked like a goldfish.

"Her hat is top secret," I said quickly. "It's made of some very special things."

Jessica smiled gratefully at me. "I can't say anything about it," she said. "Except that it's very original." She winked at me, and we both giggled.

"*My* hat was made by the famous Madame Cherie," Lila said. "Who is making your hat?"

Jessica stuck her nose up a bit, just like Lila. "The very famous Madame J," she said.

Lila scowled. "I've never heard of her," she said.

"There are probably lots of people

you haven't heard of," Jessica said with a shrug. She took her jump rope out of her backpack. "Come on, let's do double Dutch," she said, and the three of them ran off to play.

As I walked toward the school entrance, Amy Sutton came running up to me.

"Hi, Elizabeth," she said. "How's the skit going?"

I cleared my throat. "Well, I—"

"What's it going to be about this year? The Easter bunny?"

"Not exactly," I answered.

"Is it about springtime and flowers?" she asked.

"Not exactly," I said.

"Oh, I know whatever you came up with is great!" Amy said, bouncing up and down. "Please tell me what it's going to be about!"

I looked down at my sneakers. "Well, Amy, I was really busy last night. By the time I finished taking care of

Sneeches, it was bedtime," I said.

Amy looked at me, her forehead wrinkled with worry. "You mean you didn't work on the skit last night?" she asked.

"No," I said.

"Not at all?"

"Amy, I'm sorry—," I started.

"Elizabeth, today is Wednesday. We should be rehearsing the skit already," she said, chewing on her lower lip. "We'll have to write it today. Why don't you come over after school? We can both work on it this afternoon."

I thought about my baby chick, all alone in his little box, waiting for me to come home.

"I have to go home after school to take care of Sneeches," I said.

"That chicken is taking over your life," Amy complained.

"I'm sorry, Amy. Maybe you should get someone else to write the skit," I said.

"Elizabeth, everyone else already has a job for the pageant. Besides, you're the best writer in the whole second grade," Amy said. "I'll just come over to your house. Then you won't have to leave Sneeches. How about that?"

"Perfect," I said.

We walked to our classroom. Lila had a big crowd around her. Jessica was on the edge of the crowd, wearing a big frown.

"And Madame Cherie has made hats for many famous people," Lila was saying. "Even for some real princesses!"

I went over to Jessica. "Don't let her get to you," I said. "So what if she can afford to have her hat sent from Paris? The hat you make will be much better because you've made it yourself."

"I know you're right, Lizzie," Jessica said with a sigh. "But just once I'd like to have something fancy and expensive, just like Lila."

Clothes aren't that important to me, so I didn't know exactly how Jessica was feeling. But I guess it was a lot like the time Eva got selected for a special soccer demonstration and I didn't. Sometimes it's hard not to be jealous of people, even when they're your friends.

"Well, Lila may have a fancy hat with feathers," I said, grinning, "but you have something at home that has real feathers!"

That got a little smile out of Jessica. "You're right," she said. "She couldn't pay someone to make her a chicken." We both giggled.

Mrs. Otis kept us busy all day with a spelling test, a math quiz, and a science experiment. Before I knew it, it was time to go home.

"I'll have my mom drive me over," Amy called as she ran for her bus.

Jessica and I took our bus home and

had an afternoon snack. Jessica was going over to play at Lila's house.

"Now, I'll get to see what's so wonderful about that hat," Jessica told me before she got into the car with Mom.

As Mom's car left for Lila's, Amy's mom drove into our driveway. "Call me when you're ready to come home," Mrs. Sutton called to Amy. We both waved good-bye to her and then ran up my front steps.

When Amy and I got inside, Sneeches ran up to greet Amy. "Oh!" Amy said, looking frightened. "Will he peck me?"

I laughed. "A little. But it doesn't hurt," I said. As soon as the words came out of my mouth, Sneeches tottered over to peck at Amy's shoelaces.

"He must think they're worms," Amy said, watching the little chick.

"You can pet him," I said.

Amy slowly bent down and shyly began to stroke Sneeches's back.

"Sneech!" Sneeches said.

Amy jerked her hand back. "Did I hurt him?" she asked, sounding worried.

"He's fine," I said. "That means he likes you!"

Amy reached down to pet Sneeches again. "I'd hate to hear him when he doesn't like someone," she said.

"We'd better get to work," I said, scooping Sneeches up. "I thought we could work at the kitchen table. I can keep a closer eye on Sneeches in there."

Amy followed me into the kitchen. "Keep an eye on him?" she asked.

"Yeah, it was pretty exciting here this morning," I told Amy. "Sneeches tried to hitch a ride to work with Dad this morning by hiding in his briefcase."

"Hmmm," Amy said. "'The Hide-and-Seek Chick.' How's that sound for a skit?"

"Sounds great!" I said. We sat down and wrote out some ideas. Mom even agreed to let us take Sneeches to school the next day.

"He'll be great,"Amy said. "After all, he's—"

"Hello!" Jessica interrupted, walking into the kitchen. She had just come home from playing at Lila's.

"—the star," Amy finished.

"Who's the star?" Jessica asked.

"Did you get to see the famous hat from Paris?" I asked.

Jessica made a face. "Lila wants it to be a surprise for everybody. She wouldn't even give me one little peek, the rat. But never mind that, what were you talking about? Who's going to be a star?" she asked.

I giggled. "Why, you are, of course," I said, winking at Amy. Jessica loves being in the spotlight. "Amy and I hope you'll take the starring role in the skit we've written."

Amy put her hand over her mouth so Jessica wouldn't see her smile.

"Of course, I'd love to," Jessica said.

"Who am I playing? A princess? A woodland fairy? The Easter Bunny? Who? Who?"

"You get to be"—I said, smiling brightly—"a chicken."

"What?" Jessica screeched. "I don't want to be a chicken!"

I shrugged. "Then we'll just have to ask Lila," I said. "I'm sure she'll be happy to be the star of our skit."

Jessica folded her arms and frowned. "I swear, Elizabeth. You have chicken on the brain," she said.

Amy giggled. "Actually, she has chicken on the head," she said.

Sneeches, snuggled in my blond hair, agreed. "Sneech," he chirped happily.

"Oh, sneech yourself," Jessica said.

CHAPTER 10

Sneeches's Disappearing Act

The next day at school, Mrs. Otis read the play Amy and I had written.

"You've done another fabulous job," she exclaimed. "Since time is getting short, I'll give the class some time after lunch to rehearse."

"All right!" Charlie Cashman said. "No math!"

"Try not to be too disappointed, Charlie," Mrs. Otis said, smiling.

After lunch, I handed copies of the script out to everyone.

"Who's playing the lead role?" asked Lila.

"Jessica is," I said.

Charlie looked up from his script. "Jessica is the star?" he asked, laughing. "I always knew you were a ham, Jessica. But I didn't know you were a chicken, too!"

Jessica put her nose up in the air. "Lots of famous actresses have played chickens, I'll have you know," she said.

"Oh yeah?" Charlie said. "Like who?"

Jessica stuck her tongue out at Charlie.

"Places, everybody," I said, clapping my hands together. We read through the skit several times. Then we practiced acting it out. I watched, and Amy gave people their cues.

"This will be the best skit in the pageant," I said after the third time through.

"Not without costumes, it won't," Lila complained.

I clapped my hand to my mouth. I'd

totally forgotten about costumes. "Umm—," I said, thinking.

"How about bringing in things from our dress-up trunk?" suggested Jessica. "I was looking through it the other night. It's loaded with stuff we can use for costumes."

"Great idea, Jessica," I said. I looked over the script again. "We'll need some props, too."

Lila smoothed back her hair. "I'd be happy to wear my new Easter bonnet from Paris in the skit," she said.

Amy rolled her eyes.

"Uh, thanks for the offer, Lila," I said. "But I don't think it would work for your role. Horses don't usually wear hats. We'll find something for you, don't worry."

Jessica plunked down next to me. "If she says one more thing about that hat, I'll scream," she said. Every night Jessica had been trying to fix up her hat, but nothing had worked. I knew she was discouraged, but I couldn't think of anything to say to cheer her up.

"I'll just die if I don't have an Easter bonnet for the parade," Jessica said.

"You'll make it work," I said.

Jessica put her head down on her desk. "How can I decorate a hat that looks better than Lila's in one night? I give up," she said. She sounded very close to tears.

"Come on, Jess," I said. "I'll help you when we get home. We'll come up with something wonderful, OK?"

Jessica lifted her head up off the desk. "You'll really help me?" she asked.

"Of course I will," I said with a big smile. But underneath that smile, I was worried. It would take a fairy godmother to turn that old hat into an Easter bonnet.

When we got home from school that afternoon, Mom was on the phone. She was talking to Marty.

"Sneech, sneech," Sneeches called from his box. I took him out and played with him.

"We plan to be there around noon," Mom was saying.

I held Sneeches up to my cheek. A tear dropped on his little feathers. "I'm going to miss you so much," I said. He blinked up at me.

I think Sneeches could tell how sad I was. For the rest of the afternoon he followed me everywhere, sneeching in a low, quiet way.

I felt like crying, but I had to get things organized for the skit. I told Mom we needed some costumes, and she got the dress-up trunk out for me.

"Jessica, I could really use your help finding stuff to use for costumes," I said.

"But you said we'd work on my Easter bonnet," she complained.

I thought for a second. "We will. As soon as we find all the costumes." I

79

folded my hands together and knelt on the floor. "Please?" I asked.

"How can I turn you down when you ask like that?" Jessica said, throwing up her hands. "OK, let's get to work."

We both began digging through the old clothes in the trunk.

"This will work for Charlie," Jessica said, holding up a huge red-checkered handkerchief. "Farmers wear bandannas like this."

I checked that off my list. "How about something for Lila? Is there anything for a horse in here?" I asked.

Jessica rummaged around. "This long yellow scarf would work for a mane, I think," she said.

"Perfect," I said, checking it off the list. "There's one good thing about being so busy with the skit," I said. "It helps me keep my mind off Saturday."

"Saturday?" Jessica said as she tried on an old pair of lace gloves.

"You know. Taking Sneeches to Marty's farm," I said with a sigh.

Jessica patted my shoulder with a gloved hand. "It'll be okay. Don't be sad," she said.

I tried to smile. "The worst thing is I don't know how to say 'good-bye' in chicken," I said.

"Girls, dinnertime," Mom called.

My lap was covered with the clothes. I scooped them up and put them back into the trunk. "We can finish after dinner," I said.

"*And* we have to work on my bonnet," Jessica said. "You promised."

"I know, I know," I said as I followed Jessica down the hall to the dining room.

Jessica jabbered on about how wonderful her Easter bonnet was going to be and how great the skit was. I didn't feel like talking much. Not when it was nearly time to take Sneeches back to the farm.

Jessica was reciting the skit for our family. "And, then, after I say 'Here I am, the Hide-and-Seek Chick,' then Charlie says—"

"SHHHH!" Dad suddenly said, holding his finger up to his lips. "Do you hear anything?"

"Like what?" Steven asked.

"I don't hear anything," Mom said.

"I don't hear anything, either," I said.

"Are you playing a joke on us?" Jessica asked.

"No, this isn't a joke," Dad answered. "The house seems awfully quiet tonight."

"Except for Jessica," I said.

"I know what it is," Dad said. "There's no Sneeches. Is he in bed already?"

My fork froze halfway to my mouth. "Nooo," I answered slowly. I got up and went over to check his box. It was empty.

"Where is he?" Dad asked.

I realized I hadn't seen him for a

long time. "I got so busy with the skit, I forgot all about him," I said.

"You forgot about him?" Dad asked.

"Maybe he's in your briefcase again," I suggested.

He opened it up. "He's not there," he said.

I sat down at the table, my head in my hands.

"Elizabeth, where is Sneeches?" Dad asked again. He sounded worried.

"Dad, I don't know," I said, my voice cracking. "I just don't know."

CHAPTER 11

The Search for Sneeches

A huge lump got stuck in my throat. I hoped Sneeches was safe. All I needed to do was take a quick look around the kitchen to see the many dangers for a little chick.

"Well, let's not just sit here," Dad said. "Let's look for him." He stood up and began searching the kitchen. He looked behind the refrigerator and in the pantry.

"Maybe he got in one of the cupboards while Mom was cooking," Jessica said hopefully.

"I'll help you go through them," I

said, jumping up. We checked all the cupboards. He wasn't there.

"Elizabeth, you were supposed to keep an eye on him," Dad said.

"I know," I said. Tears ran down my face. "If I hadn't been so busy with those dumb costumes for that skit—" I couldn't finish the sentence. Sneeches had trusted me to take care of him. I'd let him down. And now he was lost.

Mom put her arms around me. "It's okay, honey," she said as she stroked my hair.

Dad patted my shoulder. "I'm sorry I yelled. I'm just worried about that little critter," he said.

I sniffled.

"He *has* to be in the house," Mom said.

"Let's each take a room," Dad said. "Look in every spot a little chick might hide!"

We divided up the house. I started with the living room. I pulled off the couch cushions, looked under Dad's easy chair, and behind the television. No sign of Sneeches.

Jessica came in. "I looked in the front hall closet. I went over every inch. Nothing."

We both flopped down on the couch.

"Boy, I sure hope he didn't get into the oven while Mom was cooking dinner, or hop into the clothes dryer or something like that," Jessica said.

"Oh, Jessica," I said, sobbing. "I feel terrible. Sneeches trusted me to take care of him and look what happened!" I huddled up into a little ball.

Jessica reached over and hugged me. "You didn't do it on purpose. You were just very busy working on that skit," she said.

"That stupid skit, you mean," I said bitterly.

"Don't blame yourself. The skit was important, too, and—" Jessica snapped her fingers. "That's it!" she said.

"What?" I asked.

"You spent the whole afternoon working on the skit, right?" Jessica asked. "I bet Sneeches followed you all around, just like he always does. Only you didn't pay attention because you were so busy."

I sat up. "So?" I asked.

"So, you just have to remember what you've done since you got home from school. We'll retrace your steps, and I bet you'll find Sneeches!" Jessica exclaimed.

Leaping off the couch, I grabbed my sister's arm. "You're right!" I said. "Let's go."

We ran up the stairs to our room.

"This was my first stop after school," I told Jessica. "I changed into my play clothes."

"Check the drawers!" exclaimed Jessica.

We both pounced on my dresser and

87

looked in every drawer. But there was nothing in any of them that didn't belong there, especially not a cute little chick.

"Keep looking," I told Jessica. Our bedroom was beginning to look like a hurricane had hit it. Clothes, toys, books, and hair bows were scattered everywhere.

"I don't think he's here," Jessica said finally. "Where did you go next?"

"Mom brought the dress-up trunk down to the den for me, and I started looking for costumes."

Jessica and I looked at each other. "The trunk!" I yelled. I ran back downstairs.

I nearly crashed into Dad at the bottom of the stairs. "Dad," I said, nearly out of breath. "I think I know where Sneeches is. Come on."

Dad and I raced down the hall to the den. Dad bent down in front of the open trunk and looked inside. Then he shook his head. "He's not there," he said sadly.

I knelt down beside him. I'm not sure, but I think I saw tears in his eyes.

CHAPTER 12

Safe and Sound

I sat back on my knees. I was so sure I'd find him in the trunk. Think back, Elizabeth, I told myself. I remembered getting out the scarf for Lila's costume. Right after that, Mom had called us to dinner, and then I had stuffed things back in the trunk—

"He's inside! He has to be!" I said. I started pawing through the dress-up clothes, throwing things all over the floor. There, on the very bottom, snuggled up and sleeping soundly in an old feathered hat, was—

"Sneeches!" I cried. "Dad, look. Here he is!"

Dad reached into the trunk and pulled him out.

"Sneech, sneech," he cheeped sleepily. It sounded as if he was scolding Dad for waking him up from a good dream.

"Sneech, sneech, is right," Dad said. We both started laughing and crying at the same time. "You had us worried," Dad said, cradling him close. Mom, Steven, and Jessica came running.

"Thank goodness, you've found him," Mom said.

"He almost seems proud of himself," Dad said. He kept petting Sneeches and shaking his head.

"Can we hold him, too?" Jessica asked. "You weren't the only one worried about him," she told Dad.

Dad sputtered. "Worried? I wasn't worried," he said.

Steven, Jessica, and I grinned at each other.

"I guess I've gotten very attached to that funny little chick," Dad confessed. He shrugged and looked at Mom. "I think we might have to keep him."

"I can't take him back, either," Mom said. "I'll call Marty right now and tell her we won't be coming on Saturday."

"Yay," Jessica, Steven, and I yelled.

Dad reached over to stroke Sneeches's back. "Looks like we've got our very own Hide-and-Seek Chick," he said.

CHAPTER 13

Sneeches . . . the Star!

Dad drove all of us to school the next morning—Jessica, Steven, Sneeches, and me.

"Now, make sure he has plenty of water today," Dad said. "Did you remember his food?"

"Yes, Dad," I said.

"And don't let too many kids hold him," he added. "It might tire him out. And above all—"

"Don't lose him!" Jessica and Steven finished for him.

Dad smiled. "Definitely. And did you remember the blanket? You want to make sure he's warm enough."

"Yes, Dad. You're worse than a mother hen!" I said, teasing him.

"Maybe I am getting a bit carried away," he agreed. "I just want to make sure our little chick is treated like the star he is!"

The car pulled up in front of the school, and we all piled out.

"Good luck with the skit!" Dad called after us.

We all waved as he drove off, and then hurried into school.

Before we knew it, it was show time! We got into our costumes and performed our play for the other classes. Sneeches had a big role as a baby chick. He gave a terrific performance, and we got a standing ovation.

"Wonderful job, class," Mrs. Otis said as we walked back to our classroom. She handed out bags of jelly beans to everyone. "Now it's nearly time for the Easter Bonnet Parade around the school," she said. "If you brought a bonnet, please get it now."

"Where's your bonnet, Jessica?" Lila asked as she flounced out to the coatroom.

I looked over at Jessica. She had a sad look on her face.

"Jessie, I'm sorry," I said. "We spent all our time last night either working on the skit or looking for Sneeches. We never got to finish decorating your bonnet!"

"I brought the hat, but it's no good this way," Jessica said, plunking it on her head. "Everyone will just laugh at me."

"No, they won't," I said, but the hat did look pretty awful.

Ellen came over. "Jessica, did you see Lila's hat? I've never seen anything so fancy," she said. Then she looked at Jessica's hat and burst out laughing. "What is *that*?" she asked, pointing at Jessica's head.

Jessica pulled the hat off her head and threw it on the floor. "Oh, this was something we were going to use for a costume in the skit," she said.

"That's good," Ellen said, giggling. "I was afraid you were going to wear it for the Easter Bonnet Parade."

"Heh, heh," Jessica said, forcing a laugh. "No way!" I could tell she was disappointed not to have a hat to enter.

And it was all my fault.

"And yours, too," I scolded Sneeches. "If we hadn't spent all last night trying to find you, Jessica and I would've had time to make a great hat."

"Sneech, sneech," Sneeches said and hopped over to peck at Jessica's hat. "Sneech."

I bent down to pick Sneeches up. Then it hit me!

"Sneeches, that's a brilliant idea!" I said. I grabbed Jessica. "Come on, you're going to enter your hat in that parade!" I said.

Jessica may have been the last person in the Easter Bonnet Parade, but she won first prize. After the parade, everyone crowded around her, even Lila, who was wearing her Paris bonnet and sulking.

"What a clever idea, turning the crown of the hat into a nest," Amy said.

"And those jelly beans from Mrs. Otis were a great idea, too," Eva said.

"And that yellow scarf looked just like sunshine," Julie said.

Jessica beamed. We had taken her old hat, and used some props from the skit and the jelly beans Mrs. Otis gave us to make it look like a bird's nest.

"Lila's Paris hat was kind of weird-looking, anyway," Ellen whispered so Lila wouldn't hear. "Yours really was the best, Jessica."

"You're right. After all, anybody can wear feathers in their hat—," Jessica said.

"But how many people can wear a chicken?" I said.

A fuzzy head peeked up over the crown of Jessica's bonnet. I lifted Sneeches down.

"How did you get the idea to put Sneeches in my hat?" Jessica asked me.

"A little bird told me," I said. Then we both giggled.

"Isn't that right, Sneeches?" I asked.

"Sneech," he answered. "Sneech, sneech, sneech."

"You can say that again!" Jessica exclaimed.

But Sneeches was already fast asleep in my hand.

In the puzzle below, you will find ten kinds of animals that can be found on a farm. The words are written forward, backward, and diagonally. How many can you find?

1. PIG
2. GOAT
3. COW
4. CHICKEN
5. HORSE
6. DUCK
7. ROOSTER
8. HEN
9. TURKEY
10. SHEEP

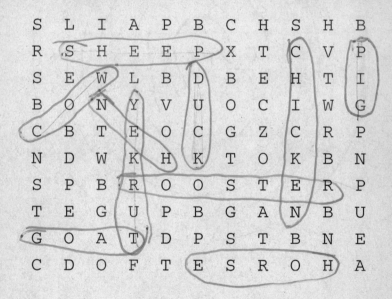

```
S  L  I  A  P  B  C  H  S  H  B
R  S  H  E  E  P  X  T  C  V  P
S  E  W  L  B  D  B  E  H  T  I
B  O  N  Y  V  U  O  C  I  W  G
C  B  T  E  O  C  G  Z  C  R  P
N  D  W  K  H  K  T  O  K  B  N
S  P  B  R  O  O  S  T  E  R  P
T  E  G  U  P  B  G  A  N  B  U
G  O  A  T  D  P  S  T  B  N  E
C  D  O  F  T  E  S  R  O  H  A
```

Help the chick find his family!

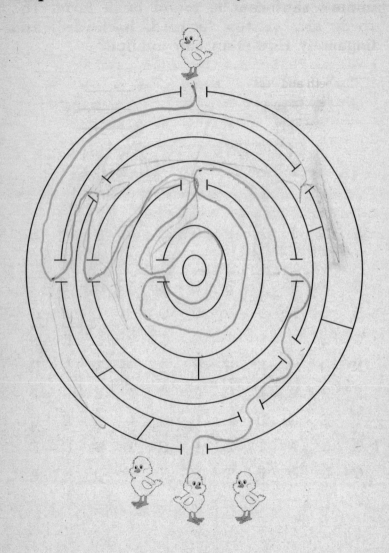

Answer the questions and then put the answers in the boxes below.

ACROSS
1. What did Elizabeth make to carry her egg in? A _____.
2. Elizabeth and Jessica's teacher is Mrs. _____.
3. Elizabeth named her baby chick _____.
4. A hat you wear for Easter is called a _____.
5. A chick has soft yellow _____.

DOWN
1. What color was the egg that Elizabeth found? _____.
2. The class had an Easter egg decorating _____.
3. The chick hid in Elizabeth's dad's _____.
4. Jessica and Elizabeth's brother is _____.
5. The twins got their costumes from the dress-up _____.

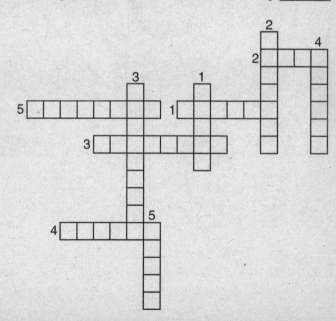

Answers

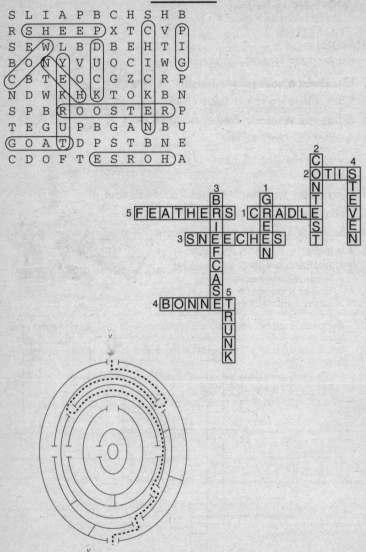

```
S L I A P B C H S H B
R S H E E P X T C V P
S E W L B D B E H T I
B O N Y V U O C I W G
C B T E O C G Z R R P
N D W K H K T O K B N
S P B R O O S T E R P
T E G U P B G A N B U
G O A T D P S T B N E
C D O F T E S R O H A
```

```
                                    ²C        ⁴
                                  ²C O T I S
³B              ¹G              N           T
⁵F E A T H E R S  ¹C R A D L E  T           E
R              E              E           V
³S N E E C H E S            N           E
E                                        N
F
C
A
⁴B O N N E T
         ⁵T
         R
         U
         N
         K
```

SIGN UP FOR THE
SWEET VALLEY HIGH®
FAN CLUB!

Hey, girls! Get all the gossip on Sweet
Valley High's® most popular teenagers
when you join our fantastic Fan Club!
As a member, you'll get all of this really
cool stuff:

- Membership Card with your own
  personal Fan Club ID number
- A Sweet Valley High® Secret
  Treasure Box
- Sweet Valley High® Stationery
- Official Fan Club Pencil (for secret
  note writing!)
- Three Bookmarks
- A "Members Only" Door Hanger
- Two Skeins of J. & P. Coats® Embroidery
  Floss with flower barrette instruction
  leaflet
- Two editions of *The Oracle* newsletter
- Plus exclusive Sweet Valley High®
  product offers, special savings,
  contests, and much more!

Be the first to find out what Jessica & Elizabeth Wakefield are up to by joining the
Sweet Valley High® Fan Club for the one-year membership fee of only $6.25 each
for U.S. residents, $8.25 for Canadian residents (U.S. currency). Includes shipping
& handling.

Send a check or money order (do not send cash) made payable to "Sweet Valley
High® Fan Club" along with this form to:

SWEET VALLEY HIGH® FAN CLUB, BOX 3919-B, SCHAUMBURG, IL 60168-3919

NAME _____
(Please print clearly)

ADDRESS _____

CITY_____ STATE _____ ZIP_____
(Required)

AGE_____ BIRTHDAY_____ /_____ /_____

Offer good while supplies last. Allow 6-8 weeks after check clearance for delivery. Addresses without ZIP
codes cannot be honored. Offer good in USA & Canada only. Void where prohibited by law.
©1993 by Francine Pascal   LCI-1383-123